Enid Blyton

A T
AFTE NO

illustrated by **Jamie Littler**

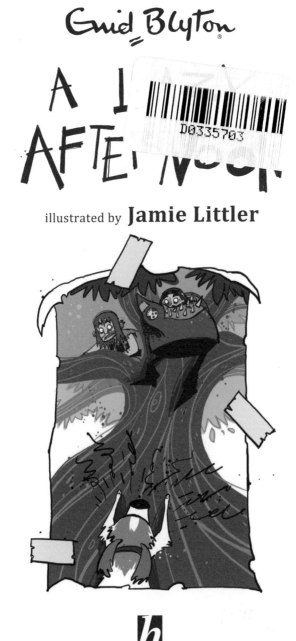

h
Hodder
Children's
Books

Famous Five Colour Reads

For a complete list of the full-length
Famous Five adventures, turn to
the last page of this book

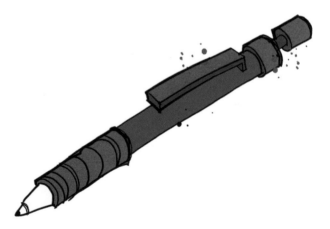

Contents

CHAPTER ONE

'**It's hot!**' said Julian, fanning himself with a paper. 'What are we all going to do this afternoon?'

'**Nothing!**' said Dick at once. 'I feel as if I'm rapidly melting. It's even **too hot** to go swimming.'

'Let's have **a lazy** afternoon for once,' said George. 'If anyone suggests a walk or a bike ride in this heat, I'll scream.'

'Woof,' said Timmy at once.

'He's suggesting a walk, George,' said Anne, with a laugh. **'Scream!'**

'Too hot even for that,' said George. 'Let's find a cool, shady place, take our books, and either read or snooze till tea-time. I'd enjoy a lazy afternoon for once.'

'Woof,' said Timmy mournfully, not agreeing at all.

'Come on, then,' said Julian. 'We'll go to that **little copse** we know, under those leafy trees – near that tiny stream that ripples along and makes a nice **cool** noise!'

THE FAMOUS FIVE
SHORT STORIES

A LAZY AFTERNOON

The Famous Five

Timmy   Anne   Dick   Julian   George

HODDER CHILDREN'S BOOKS

Text first published in Great Britain in *Enid Blyton's Magazine Annual – No. 1* in 1954
This edition first published in Great Britain in 2014 by Hodder & Stoughton
14

A CIP catalogue record for this book is available from the British Library.

ISBN 978 1 444 91629 4

Printed in China

The paper and board used in this book are made from wood from responsible sources.

MIX
Paper from
responsible sources
FSC® C104740
www.fsc.org

Hodder Children's Books
An imprint of Hachette Children's Group
Part of Hodder and Stoughton
Carmelite House 50 Victoria Embankment London EC4Y 0DZ

An Hachette UK Company
www.hachette.co.uk
www.hachettechildrens.co.uk

'Well – I think I can just about walk there,' said Dick, and they all set off, strolling along, unable to keep up with the lively, energetic Timmy.

'It makes me hot even to look at Timmy,' complained Dick. 'Hot to hear him too, puffing like a steam-train. Put your tongue in, Timmy, I can't bear to look at it.'

CHAPTER TWO.

Timmy ran ahead, glad that they were off for what appeared to be a walk. He was **very disappointed** when the others **flopped down** in a little copse under some big leafy trees near a small brook. He stood looking at them in disgust.

'Sorry, Tim. **No walkies,'** said George. 'Come and sit down with us. For goodness' sake, **don't go rabbiting** in this weather.'

'It'd be a waste of your time, Timmy,' said Dick. 'All sensible bunnies are having an afternoon snooze, down at the bottom of their holes, waiting for the cool evening to come.'

'Woof,' said Timmy in scorn, watching the four arrange themselves comfortably under a canopy made by young saplings and bushes.

Branches from big trees nearby overhung them, and by the time the four had wriggled themselves well into the little thicket, not a single sunbeam could reach them. In fact, it was **difficult to see them**, so well **hidden were they** in the **green shade**.

'This is better,' said George. 'I think it's about the coolest spot we'll find anywhere. Doesn't that little stream sound nice, too, gurgling away over the stones. I think I'm going to sleep – and if you dare to flop yourself down on my middle, Timmy, I'll send you home!'

Timmy stood and looked at
the **well-hidden four.**

His tail drooped.

What was the point of coming to a wood,
to lie down and do nothing? Well – **he was
going rabbiting!** He swung
round, pushed his way out
of the thicket, and
disappeared.

George raised her head to look after him.

'He's gone rabbiting after all,' she said. 'Well, I hope he remembers where we are and comes back at tea-time. Now for **a lazy** – **peaceful** – **quiet afternoon!'**

'Don't talk so much,' said Dick, and got a sideways kick from George's foot.

'Oh, I feel *sleepy!'*

CHAPTER THREE

In a few minutes' time **not one** of the four **was awake.**

Books lay unopened on the ground.

A small beetle ran over Anne's bare leg,
and she **didn't** even **feel it.**

A robin hopped on to a branch just above Dick's face, but his eyes were closed and he **didn't** see it.

It certainly was a hot afternoon. **Nobody** was about at all. **Not a sound** was to be heard except for the running water nearby,

and a yellowhammer
somewhere who persisted
in saying that he wanted
'a little bit of bread
and no cheese'.
The four were as
sound **asleep**
as if they were in bed.

And then, far away on a road that bordered the wood, **a motorbike** came by. It had a sidecar, and it made **quite a noise.**

But the
four sleepers
heard nothing.

They didn't know that the motorbike had slowed down and **turned into the wood,**

taking one of the grassy woodland walks that wound here and there, quiet and cool.

The motorbike
came slowly down
one of the paths,

not making
very much
noise now,
because it was
going slowly.

It came near to the little copse where the **children lay hidden** in the cool shade of the bushes.

The engine of the motorbike gave a sudden little *cough* as it came along, and Julian awoke with a start.

What was that noise? He listened, but he could hear nothing more because the motorbike, with its sidecar, **had now stopped.**

Julian shut his eyes again. But he opened them immediately because he **heard voices** – low voices. People must be somewhere near. Where were they? Julian hoped they wouldn't disturb the four in their cool hiding place. He made a little **peephole** in the bush he was lying under, and **spied** through it.

CHAPTER FOUR

Julian saw the **motorbike** and **sidecar** on the grassy path some way off. He saw **two men,** one just getting out of the sidecar. Julian didn't like the look of them at all.

'What **nasty-looking men!'**
he thought. 'What are they doing here in
the middle of a summer's afternoon?'

At first the men talked in low voices,
and then an argument started. One raised
his voice.

'I tell you, **we were
followed!** It's the only thing to do, to
come here and **dump the stuff!'**

A **small bag** was dragged out of
the sidecar. The second man seemed
to be grumbling, not at all willing to
do what the other wanted.

'I tell you, I know it **won't be found** if we put it **there,'** said the first man. 'What's the matter with you? We can't afford to be stopped with **the stuff on us –**

and I know we were **being followed.**
It was only because we crossed against
those traffic lights that we got away.'

Julian awoke the others, and whispered to them. **Something strange** was happening!

Soon all the four were **peeping through leafy peepholes** at what was going on.

They saw what looked like a **small mailbag** on the ground by the motorbike.

'What are they going to do with it?' whispered George. 'Should we burst out on them?'

'I would if we had **Timmy** with us,' whispered back Julian. 'But he's gone rabbiting and may be **miles away.'**

'And these crooks would be more than a match for us,' said Dick. 'We **daren't** even **show ourselves.** We can only watch.'

CHAPTER FIVE

'I hope we see where they hide the stuff, whatever it is,' said Anne, trying to spy through the leaves. 'There they go with the bag.'

'**I can see them,**' said Dick, almost forgetting to whisper in his excitement. '**They're climbing a tree!**'

'Yes – one's already up, and the other's **passing the bag** to him,' whispered Julian. 'It must have a **hollow trunk,** I think. Oh, I wish Timmy was here!'

'Now the second man's trying to climb up, too,' said George. 'The first one wants help, I suppose. **The bag must be stuck.'**

Both men were now up the tree, trying to **stuff the bag** down some kind of **hollow** there. At last there was **a thud** as if **the bag** had **dropped** down.

'If only **Timmy was here!**' said Julian again. 'It's maddening to lie here and **do nothing –** but we'd be no match for those two men!'

Then a sudden noise came to their ears – the **scampering of feet.** Then came a familiar sound. **'Woof!'**

'Timmy!' yelled Julian and George together, and Julian leapt up and pushed his way out of his hiding place at once. 'Tell Tim to **guard** that **tree,** George, quick!'

CHAPTER SIX

'Here, Timmy – **on guard!**' shouted
George, and the astonished Timmy ran to the
tree where the two men were staring down in
sudden horror.

and one man, who had
been about to jump
down, shrank back.

'Call that dog off!' he yelled. 'What do you think you're doing?'

'You tell us what *you're* doing,' said Julian. 'What's in the bag you pushed down that tree hollow?'

'What bag? What are you talking about? You must be mad!' said the man. **'Call that dog off,** or I'll **report you** to the **police.'**

'Right! We'll report you at the **same time!'** said Julian. 'You'll stay up that tree till we bring the police back here – and I warn you, if you try jumping down and running away, you'll be sorry. You've no idea what **sharp teeth** that dog has!'

The two men were **so angry** that they could hardly speak. Timmy **barked** loudly, and kept **leaping up** to try to reach them.

Julian turned to the others. 'Go to the main road and stop a car. Go to the nearest police station and tell the police there to send men here at once. Hurry up.'

But before the others could go off, there came the sound of **another motorbike** – and then **a second** – bumping along the woodland path. Julian fell silent. Were more crooks coming? Timmy would be a great help, if so. Julian and the others got behind trees and watched to see who was on the coming motorbikes.

CHAPTER SEVEN

'**The police!**' yelled Dick, suddenly
seeing the familiar uniform. 'They must have
been the ones **chasing those men.** Somebody
must have given them the tip that they had
turned off into the wood!
    Hey! We can help you!'

The two policemen stopped in surprise.

They saw the motorbike and sidecar.

'Have you kids **seen** anything of **two men with a bag?**' shouted one of them.

'Yes. **The bag's stuffed down a tree over there, and our dog's guarding the men** – they're **up in the tree!'** shouted back Julian, going towards the police. 'You've just come in time to collect them!'

'Good stuff!' said the policeman with a grin, as he saw the two scared men up the tree, **with Timmy still leaping up** hopefully at them. 'The bag's up there, too, is it?'

'Down in the hollow of the tree,' said Julian.

'Well, thanks very much for doing our job for us,' said the second policeman. 'We've got some pals on the main road,' he said. 'We said we'd shout if we found anything. They'll soon be along.' He looked at the two men in the tree. 'Well, Jim and Stan? You thought you'd fooled us, didn't you? Are you coming quietly – or do we ask the dog to help us round you up?'

CHAPTER EIGHT

Jim and Stan took one look at the
eager Timmy.

'We'll come quietly,' they said, and,
when three more men came racing down the
woodland path, there was no trouble at all.

Jim and Stan went off with the policemen, Timmy gave **one last fierce bark,** and all Five watched the men, the motorbikes, and the sidecar disappear with many bumps up the path back to the main road.

'Well!' said George. 'Talk about a nice cool, **lazy afternoon!** I'm **hotter** than ever now!'

'Woof,' said Timmy, his tongue hanging out almost to the ground. He looked very hot, too.

'Well, you shouldn't go rabbiting,' said George. 'No wonder you're hot!'

'It's a very good thing he did go rabbiting!' said Dick. 'If he'd been with us, he'd have barked, and those men would have known we were here – and would have gone further on to hide their goods. We'd never have seen what they were doing, or have been able to catch them.'

'Yes. That's true,' said George, and patted Timmy. 'All right, Timmy – you were right to go rabbiting and to come back when you did!'

'Tea-time, everybody!'

said Dick, looking at his watch.

'Well – what a very nice, peaceful,
**lazy afternoon!
I really have enjoyed it!'**

If you enjoyed this Famous Five short story, there's plenty more action and adventure in the full-length Famous Five novels. Here is a list of all the titles, in the order they were first published.

1. Five On A Treasure Island
2. Five Go Adventuring Again
3. Five Run Away Together
4. Five Go to Smuggler's Top
5. Five Go Off in a Caravan
6. Five On Kirrin Island Again
7. Five Go Off to Camp
8. Five Get Into Trouble
9. Five Fall Into Adventure
10. Five on a Hike Together
11. Five Have a Wonderful Time
12. Five Go Down to the Sea
13. Five Go to Mystery Moor
14. Five Have Plenty of Fun
15. Five on a Secret Trail
16. Five Go to Billycock Hill
17. Five Get Into a Fix
18. Five on Finniston Farm
19. Five Go to Demon's Rocks
20. Five Have a Mystery to Solve
21. Five Are Together Again